CW00842014

FATHER CHRISTMAS'

LONDON.
F. WARNE & C°
AND NEW YORK.
[ALL RIGHTS RESERVED]

The facsimile

FATHER CHRISTMAS' ABC

A facsimile of the original edition

Bodleian Library
UNIVERSITY OF OXFORD

First published in 2005 by the Bodleian Library
Broad Street, Oxford, OX1 3BG

ISBN 1 85124 325 9

Copyright © Bodleian Library, University of Oxford

Designed by Melanie Gradtke
Printed and bound by Butler and Tanner, Frome, Somerset
A catalogue record for this book is available from the British Library

A facsimile from two copies in the Bodleian Library:
John Johnson, Alphabets 2 and 2523 c.17

FATHER CHRISTMAS' ABC

A is for Apples, that Auntie will bring .

B for the Bells, that at Christmas-time ring:

C for the Cracker that Kate pulls with Fred,

D for our Doggie with cap on his head:

E for an Envelope bringing good wishes,

F for the Fruit mamma puts in the dishes:

G for our Games and our Gambols so jolly,

H for the badge of Old Christmas, the Holly.

I is the Ice, on which skaters dart:

J is the Jam Jane puts in the tart.

K for sweet Kisses 'neath Mistletoe snatched:

L is for Luggage by quick train despatched.

A is for Apples
That Auntie will bring:

B for the Bells
That at Christmas-time ring.

C for the Cracker
That Kate pulls
with Fred.

D for our Doggie
With cap on his head.

E for an Envelope
Bringing good wishes:

F for the Fruit
Mamma puts in the dishes

G for our Games
and our Gambols so jolly.

H for the badge of Old Christmas
the Holly.

I is the Ice
On which skaters dart.

J is the Jam
Jane puts in a tart.

JAM

STRAWBERRY JAM

K for sweet Kisses
Neath Mistletoe snatche

L for the Luggage
    By quick train despatched.

M is for Mince Pies
All sugar and plums.

N for Nutcrackers
    For saving our gums.

O is for Orange
Good, eaten
in reason.

P for Plum Pudding
The crown of the Season.

Q is the Quadrille
Danced at our party.

R for the Reindeer
Of Santa Claus hearty.

S for the Stocking
That Santa Claus fills.

T for the
Toys

That cure all our ills.

U is an Umbrella
To keep off the snow

V are the Visitors
Kind friends we know.

W is a Waggon
Laden with Ho

X is for Xmas tree
All light, and toys jolly.

Y are the Youngsters
Who welcome the
Christmas-time

and Z is a Zany
A clown at a Pantomime.

M is for Mince pies, all sugar and plums,

N for Nutcrackers for saving our gums

O is for Orange, good, eaten in reason

P for Plum Pudding the crown of the season

Q is the Quadrille, danced at our party,

R for the Reindeer of Santa Claus heart

S for the Stocking that Santa Claus fill

T for the Toys that cure all our ills.

U is an Umbrella to keep off the snow:

V are the Visitors, kind friends we know.

W is a Waggon, laden with Holly

X is for Xmas tree, all lights, and toys joll

Y are the Youngsters, who welcome the Christmas-tim

and **Z** is a Zany, a clown at a Pantomime.